This book belongs to...

_____

ALLEY DOGS

Water Hunt

Bright ☆ Sparks

This is a Bright Sparks Book
First published in 2000
BRIGHT SPARKS, Queen Street House, 4 Queen Street, Bath BA1 1HE, UK

Copyright © PARRAGON 2000

Created and produced by THE COMPLETE WORKS,
St. Mary's Road, Royal Leamington Spa, Warwickshire CV31 1JP, UK

Editorial Director: Mike Phipps
Project Manager: Stuart Branch
Editor: Aneurin Rhys
Designer: Anne Matthews

ISBN 1-84250-010-4

ALLEY DOGS

Water Hunt

Written by Lesley Rees
Illustrated by Terry Burton

Bright ☆ Sparks

In the tumble-down, messy alley it was a *very* hot day. Harvey and his gang were melting!

"I need a slurpy, slippy popsicle," Ruffles sighed.

"I need a cool pool to roll in," Puddles squeaked.

Those hot dogs just didn't know what to do!

"It's even too hot to sleep," complained Bonnie. "I'm the hottest dog in the whole world!"

"I bet I'm hotter than you!" snorted Ruffles.

"Oh no, you're not," replied Patchy. "I am!"

"I haven't been this hot," said Mac, "since I was in the desert when…"

"*Not now, Mac*!" the other dogs all yelled together.

"Stop!" cried Harvey. "It's much too hot to argue! Listen, I know what we'll do…"

"Let's play a game. Let's have a—water hunt."

"Can I hunt, too?" yelped Puddles, hopping from one hot paw to the other.

"Do we have to move, Harvey?" groaned Patchy. "I don't think I can."

"Come on," said Harvey. "Where can we find some water?"

"I'm too hot to think," wailed Bonnie.

"We're too hot to do *anything*," said Patchy.

"Except gobble down yummy ice cold ice cream," replied Ruffles, with a grin.

"I know," cried Mac suddenly. "Let's go to the beach! We could play in the sand and splish and splash in the water."

"Good thinking, Mac," smiled Harvey. "But it's too far for us to go on a day like today. Can you think of something else?"

"I've got a *real* good idea," said Ruffles.

"What is it?" asked Bonnie.

"Diggin'!" Ruffles grinned.

"Digging?" cried the others. "Dig for water in this heat?"

"No," said Ruffles excitedly. "Dig for bones. The dirt will be damp and cool and we could roll around in it and…"

"No way, Ruffles," said Harvey firmly. "Today is *not* a digging day."

"Let's go to the park," suggested Patchy. "We could jump in and out of the wading pool and play in the fountain."

Poor Puddles looked as though she were going to burst into tears.

"I can't walk that far, Harvey," she whispered. "I've only got small legs!"

"Don't worry, Puddles," said Harvey kindly. "We won't go without you."

"Oh, there *must* be some water somewhere!" Patchy puffed and panted.

"If I don't find water soon, I'm going to melt into a big, hairy puddle!" groaned Ruffles.

"Haven't you got *any* ideas at all, Harvey?" asked Mac.

But even Harvey was too hot to think, and Bonnie had given up and had gone to sleep in her trash can!

Those poor hot dogs — what in the world could they do?

Meanwhile, the sizzling Alley Cats were searching, too. But they weren't on a water hunt. No! They were on a mouse hunt — Archie had lost his favorite toy mouse!

"I WANT IT BACK!" wailed Archie, looking under a box.

"It's not in here!" called Bertie from the top of a flower pot.

"Phew!" Hattie groaned. "It's way too hot for hunting, Archie. Why don't we have a cat nap instead?"

"Cat nap time!" said Lucy. "Great idea."

So the Alley Cats snuggled down for an afternoon nap — or did they?

Lenny and Lulu — the two little kittens — weren't quite ready for a nap just yet!

"Naps are for babies," whispered Lenny to his sister. "Come on, Lulu, follow me."

"Yippee!" Lulu giggled. "An adventure."

The kittens clambered and climbed over the pots and pans and headed towards a hole in the fence.

"Hey, Lulu!" cried Lenny. "I bet we find Archie's mouse through here."

So, carefully and quietly, the kittens squeezed themselves through the tiny gap…

Suddenly, a strange, stripey monster jumped out in front of them!

"AAAAAGH!" screamed Lulu. "What is it?"

Swooping and swaying through the spikey grass, the monster wiggled and wiggled towards them. Then it lifted up its head and gave a loud, angry "HISSSSS!"

"It's a snake!" yelled Lenny. "Let's vamoose."

Running as fast as they could, the kittens bounded towards a tree trunk and scampered up into its branches!

"We'll be safe up here," Lenny gasped.

But Lenny was wrong!

The sinister snake hissed louder and louder and slithered up the tree after them.

Lenny and Lulu quivered and quaked.

"HELP!" they wailed.

As the snake swayed about in front of the kittens, the poor little pussies began to cry.

With one, last enormous "HISSSSSSS!", the swinging snake leapt towards them—and got stuck in a branch!

Suddenly a great big spurt of water gushed from the snake's mouth, shot over the fence and into the alley below — SPLOSH!

Those silly scally wags. It wasn't a snake at all. It was a hosepipe and the cool refreshing water woke up Harvey and the gang. They couldn't believe their eyes!

"It's rainy and sunny at the same time," Harvey laughed.

He looked up and saw Lenny and Lulu peeping shyly over the fence.

"You clever cats," he called up to them.

"Let's give a cheer for Lenny and Lulu!" cried Harvey. "HOORAY! HOORAY! HOORAY!"

And so, two cool cats had made six hot dogs very happy!

The End

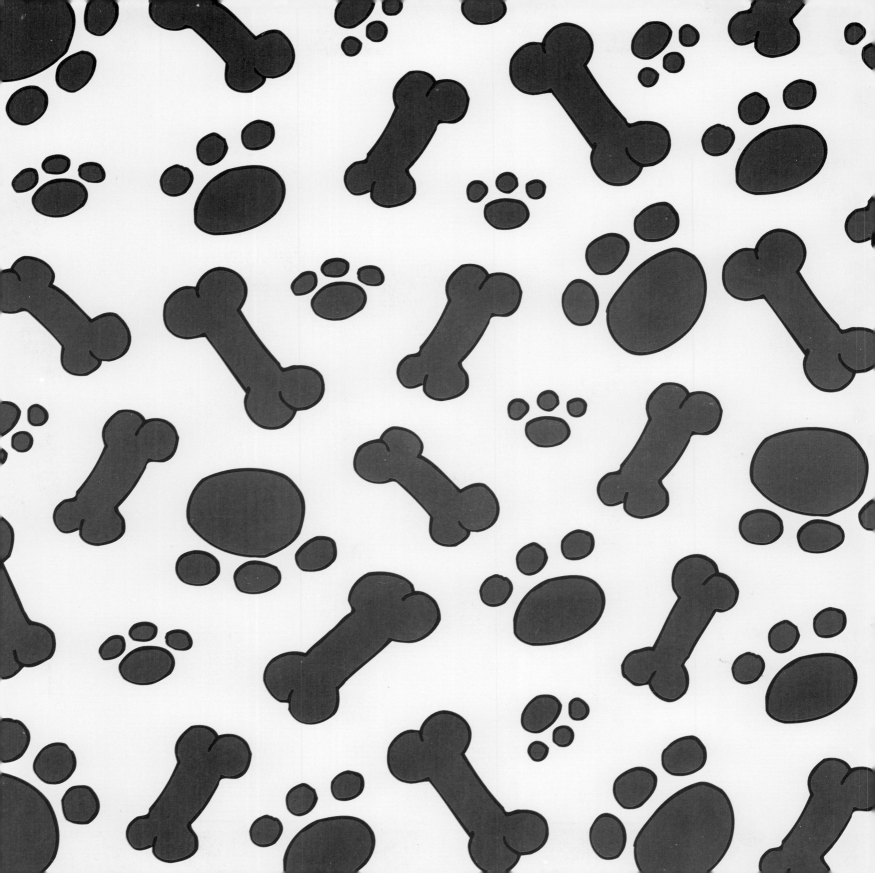